blueside up

an angel among us

blueside up

an angel among us

Inspired by actual events

by T.J. Martini

First Printing January 2005

Layout and Design: Jay Degn, Reno, Nevada
Editor: Melissa Van Vuuren, Bloomington, Indiana
Concept: Gary Lebeck, Reno, Nevada
Cover Design: Donald Zimmerman, Reno, Nevada

Photograph of T.J. Martini: Spicer Photography, Reno, Nevada
Photograph of Kristin Mills: Steven Shofner Photography, Las Vegas, Nevada

Pictures in Kristin's Photo Album courtesy of Gene and Leslie Batdorf,
Larry and Dawn Germain and Dave Mills.

Scripture taken from the *Holy Bible*,
New International Version® Copyright ©. 1973, 1978, 1984
by International Bible Society.
Used by permission of Zondervan Publishing House. All rights reserved.

New King James Version Copyright ©. 1979, 1980, 1982 by Thomas Nelson, Inc.
Used by permission. All rights reserved.

Printed in the United States of America
10 9 8 7 6 5 4 3 2 1

Vaughan Printing - Nashville, Tennessee

Library of Congress Cataloging–in–Publication Data

Martini, T. J., 1948–
    Blue side up : an angel among us : inspired by actual events / by T.J. Martini.
    p. cm.
ISBN 0–9705018–3–8 (alk. paper)
I. Title.
PS3613.A787B58 2004
813'.6--dc22

                        2004022627

Contents

Acknowledgments

Not many people realize the amount of work involved in writing a book, even a small one like *Blue Side Up*. It takes a great deal of time, patience, research, and prayer to get it to each stage. The success of these stages would be impossible without the Lord's amazing grace, and because of His grace, He guided me to all of you. For weeks on end, you made yourselves available to me. In the end you all willingly, joyfully, and systematically came together and made this book a reality. I want to thank each one of you personally for your overwhelming support, incredible ideas, hours of assistance, and never–ending prayers, for without each of you this book would not have been possible. I am so grateful.

First and foremost, I want to thank my Lord and Savior Jesus Christ for His incredible gift of life and for providing me with all I need to carry out His plan and accomplish my dreams and His purpose. I thank you, Gary Lebeck, my husband and partner, for your insight into and concept for every project we share. Your ideas never cease to amaze me! Thank you, Jay Degn, for giving me your precious time to do the layout design even in the midst of all your challenges. Thank you, Jeff Spicer of Spicer Photography in Reno for your incredibly skillful eye, and to Leah Witt and Carol Dearing for the countless hours you both spent making corrections and suggestions. Thank you, Melissa Van Vuuren, for the final edit and for making sure everything came together perfectly. You all make me look better than I know I am! And to Donald Zimmerman, thank you so much for all your time spent designing the beautiful cover for this book. It is exactly how I envisioned it would be.

And to you, Dave Mills, thank you for sharing your memories of those last few days with your wife. I know how painful it must have been for you, and I appreciate your time and input. Also, a very special thank you to the amazing family of Kristin Mills: her parents, Gene and Leslie Batdorf, and her brother–in–law and nephew, Larry and Daniel Germain. Your loss is unimaginable. I commend all of you for your strength, your courage, and your faithfulness to God, even now.

And last but certainly not least, I thank you, Dawn

Germain! When I started gathering information for *Blue Side Up*, I didn't know you. To this day we have never met in person, though I pray that someday we will. God knew exactly what He was doing when He led me to you. Without your determination, loyalty, and incredibly open and willing heart, this book could not have been completed. You have been my eyes, ears, hands, and feet. You were always there for anything and everything I needed. There were no limits when it came to providing me with all the facts, names, and figures needed to put this book together. Since I began the research on this book in late 2002, you and I have spent hours on the phone talking about the remarkable woman your sister was and of the accident that took her away. Now I can hardly go a day without hearing your voice! Over these last few months, I fell in love with you, Dawn, first as a sister in Christ and now as a very dear friend. Whether we ever meet in this lifetime is of God's choosing, but I know I will cherish the long distance memories forever.

Thank you all so much. May the Lord be with you always!

For Kristin

Prologue

JANUARY 8, 2000

12:30 P.M.

"My, aren't we trying to be intellectual, and so early in the day," Dawn said to her sister teasingly. "What are you reading?"

"It's a book called *Chocolate for a Woman's Soul!* It's really awesome, Dawn, full of all these different inspirational stories from people all around the world," Kristin said, holding up her copy. "Each story really touches your heart and is meant to satisfy the soul like chocolate does when you eat it."

"It sounds sort of like the one I have," Dawn answered, reaching for her own book. "Mine's called *Chicken Soup for the Christian Soul*. The stories in the book are intended to heal like chicken soup does when you're sick."

"Yeah, I've heard of that one. But look! Mine's autographed by the lady who wrote it. See, right there? Signed by Kay Allenbaugh," the younger sister announced proudly. "Kay was on one of my flights back in 1997, and she gave it to me. She said I have a contagious smile. And, of course, we know it's true," Kristin giggled.

The sisters sat on the couch comparing many of the stories inside each of their books. They laughed and joked around as they always did whenever they were together. It was as if time had gone backwards and they were still allowed to be silly young girls.

"Kristin," their mother interrupted, "don't you think you'd better get ready to go? Your plane leaves in less than two hours."

"Oh, I suppose I should. Are you taking me to the airport, or is Dawn?"

"We both are," Dawn informed her.

Kristin went into the guest bedroom of her sister's house in Sequim, Washington, where she quickly packed her belongings into a small overnight case. She hated leaving again so soon, but she had to be back in Seattle by early morning. It was only a 25–minute flight on Horizon Air. This particular airline used a small 30–seat commuter plane that Kristin referred to as a "puddle jumper." Because of its size, she only flew on it when it was absolutely necessary. Kristin had only one day to spend with her family this time, and it was faster and more convenient to take the commuter flight than it was to drive.

She had just put the last of her things inside her suitcase, when suddenly from out of nowhere Kristin had a frightening vision and began to panic. Her body shook and her voice quivered.

"I can't go. I just can't," she whispered out loud. "I'm scared. I just know something terrible is going to happen." Kristin sat on the edge of the bed. Her hands covered her face as she wept.

Dawn heard her sister talking from the next room and came running. She was caught completely off guard by

Kristin's emotional state. It was so unlike her to be afraid about anything, but especially about flying. She was a flight attendant, for heaven's sake.

"What are you talking about?" the older sibling asked curiously. Though Kristin was known to be a bit dramatic at times, Dawn had never seen her act this way. "What's the matter with you? It never bothered you to fly on these planes before. Why are you being so weird?"

"I don't know. I saw something. It was just for a minute, but I saw something. I just have a really uneasy feeling. I can't get on this plane. I just know something bad is going to happen." Kristin looked up into her sister's eyes. Her fear was very evident and very real. "Dawn, tell me the truth. Do you think it's going to crash?"

"Of course it isn't. Why would you even think that way?" her mother, Leslie, interrupted as she walked into the room.

"I'm just scared, Mom, really scared. That's all. I don't know why. I hate those small planes. Do you think something bad will happen?" she asked again.

"Of course I don't. But, Kristin, what if someday something bad does happen? Can you honestly tell me that you'll be ready to go?" Her mother was clear on her meaning. It pained Leslie even to think that Kristin might not be ready.

Kristin knew exactly what her mother meant. She wasn't asking whether her affairs were in order. She was asking about the readiness of her spirit and where she would spend eternity. Leslie worried constantly about Kristin's relationship with God, and with good reason. Her daughter hadn't been very strong or faithful in her Christian walk lately. In fact, Kristin had been struggling off and on for several years.

"Yeah, I guess I'm ready. But why would you say that? You think the plane is going to crash, don't you?" Kristin just couldn't let it go.

"It isn't going to crash, Kristin. But if you're so concerned, I'll just drive you back to Seattle," Dawn finally told her. "It will only take a few hours. I don't mind, really."

"No, I'll be okay. Let's just go before I change my mind."

Dawn and Leslie drove Kristin to the airport in Port Angeles without incident. And just like they hoped, she was fine as soon as she got on the plane. When Kristin got home to Seattle, she called Dawn as promised.

"I'm sorry I acted that way. I don't know what came over me. It was silly, I know," she said, a bit embarrassed. "Tell Mom I made it back and that I'm sorry, okay?"

"It's okay. We're all allowed to get a little weird once in a while. I'm glad you made it home safely. I'll tell Mom you called. Call me when you get back from your trip. I love you, Pooh," Dawn said sweetly.

"I love you, too. Oh, and Dawn, tell Mom not to worry. I know I haven't been a very good Christian lately, but I promise I'll be ready when it's time."

"I'll tell her. But better yet, why don't you show her!"

"I might just do that, Piglet. Talk to you soon," Kristin said and hung up the phone.

Chapter One
From Alaska to Las Vegas

Kristin Rochelle Batdorf was born January 11, 1974, in Ketchikan, Alaska. She lived there with her parents, Gene and Leslie, and her older sister, Dawn, for more than twelve years. Gene and Leslie Batdorf were God–fearing Christians, and they raised their daughters to be the same.

From a very early age, Kristin attended church where she learned about God and Heaven and the awesome power of prayer. She began praying for everything, but especially for those less fortunate than herself. She knew that God had a special plan for her someday, and she was anxious for Him to reveal it.

On June 18, 1984, during a Nazarene Church summer camp, Kristin willingly and gratefully accepted Jesus Christ as her Savior. She was, indeed, a child of God. For one so young, she truly understood the meaning of John 3:16 that "God so loved the world that He gave His only Son, so that everyone who believes in Him will not perish, but have eternal life." Kristin knew the only way to be one of God's children was to believe in His Son, Jesus. And she did, with all her heart.

Kristin believed and loved more than most kids her age. Though she was young, she was very eager to please, not only her Maker but also everyone around her. There wasn't anything she wouldn't do for a family member, a friend, or even a stranger. In fact, in Kristin's world there were no strangers, only friends she hadn't met yet.

As a child, Kristin had one dream and one passion. Her dream was to be a flight attendant and to someday work for Alaska Airlines. Because of her desire to please and serve, Kristin thought that being a flight attendant would suit her personality perfectly. Her passion was to dance. Kristin would perform in front of anybody who would watch. She loved being the center of attention and was not the least bit shy. Those who watched were always amazed at how natural dancing came for her and how talented she really was.

Her childhood prayer was that someday she would be able to be both a flight attendant and a dancer. But in true Kristin fashion, she left her future in the hands of God. She would have to wait and see what His plan was for her.

In 1987, Gene and Leslie took their youngest daughter and moved to exciting Las Vegas, Nevada. Dawn and her new husband, Larry Germain, were already living there. They all felt blessed to be together once again, but as Kristin got further into her teens, her family began to notice the change.

The once straight and narrow path Kristin had been on as a child suddenly took a sharp turn in the wrong direction. The carefree teenager developed a somewhat wild spirit, which made it impossible to keep her grounded. Her lust for life and fun became apparent to all who knew her. The older Kristin got, the further away she drifted, as she got caught up in the twenty-four hour southern Nevada lifestyle. Her family often referred to her as the prodigal daughter. They were desperate for a happy ending and maintained high hopes that she'd come back just like the prodigal son in the Bible. (Luke 15:11–32.)

Though Kristin was still a caring Christian, it was

obvious that her priorities had changed. Her family prayed constantly for her rebellious nature to run its course, but they knew it wouldn't come easy! God definitely had His work cut out for Him. Kristin was growing into a very beautiful young woman with big, blue angelic eyes, long, strawberry blonde hair, and a smile that was known to melt even the hardest of hearts.

Kristin struggled through her early twenties, trying hard to please her family yet still wanting to experience life to its fullest. She craved it. It was almost as if she knew she had to experience everything as quickly as possible before life passed her by.

Kristin still prayed and believed, but there were too many times that it was easier and much more exciting to be the life of the party. And that she was! Even when attempting to minister to her closest friends, Kristin had to do it her way. She would often invite people over to her apartment. Then she would serve appetizers and margaritas while sharing the Gospel with them. She knew for some that this could very well be the only spiritual message they would ever hear. Her "margarita" Bible studies became quite popular among her inner circle. Even in their clouded state of mind, no one ever seemed offended when she shared with them the teachings of God. And because God had given Kristin an exceptionally kind heart many years before, it made her so easy to believe and to love. No matter where she was or what she was doing, the young woman was like a life–size magnet. People were immediately drawn to her. Her enthusiasm, high energy, and free spirit mixed with kindness, understanding, and love were too much for anyone to ignore.

Often Kristin found herself lost in an environment of worldly excitement, which was just where Satan wanted her. But her Heavenly Father never gave up on her. She was His and always would be. But His plan for her was coming to fruition, and He needed her back.

It was obvious that a spiritual war was brewing in Kristin's world, as sometimes happens when a great plan is in effect for one of God's children. The war was keeping Kristin away from many things she knew to be right. There were days when she was too far away to hear His voice, and she wasn't spiritually strong enough to fight back. As a result, she was left with very little armor to shield her from the enemy.

But God continued to whisper in her ear, or tug on

her heart to get her attention. Sometimes He resorted to tougher measures, leaving Kristin brokenhearted, confused, and in tears. But through it all there was never a time that she did not feel His love. She never once lost her faith nor stopped believing. Everyone was sure that something big was going to happen to Kristin someday. Deep down, Kristin knew it too!

Chapter Two
A DREAM COME TRUE

Kristin's first opportunity at her childhood dream came in late 1996, when the Nevada–based airline, Reno Air, hired her as one of their flight attendants. She was living in Las Vegas at the time with her new husband and high school sweetheart, Dave Mills. Reno Air had just opened a new domicile in Las Vegas, which was where Kristin would be based. She loved her job immediately.

Kristin decided to put her dream of professional dancing aside for good. Though she still loved to dance, Kristin settled for it being more of hobby for her own enjoyment. Besides, she had a feeling that being a flight attendant would someday play a part in God's plan and purpose for her, and she wanted to be ready. Though her walk was shaky much of the time, Kristin trusted God to guide her where He wanted her to be, no matter what she was doing in her life.

For nearly three years, Kristin enjoyed all the perks of her job with Reno Air. Working for an airline allowed her and her husband, as well as many of her family members and friends, the freedom to travel all over the country at very little expense. This was truly her dream come true. Her dream was not only to explore new places but also to surround herself with people for whom she cared so deeply. After a while, Kristin began thinking less about her childhood fantasy of working for Alaska Airlines. Maybe it was just not meant to be. Because of her love for everyone at Reno Air, she could not imagine ever wanting to leave.

Kristin loved all of her colleagues, and they absolutely adored her. How could they not? She brought with her a ray of sunshine no matter where she was or what she was doing. She never seemed to have a bad day, or if she did, she never let it show. Kristin made it a priority never to be a part of any gossip and never said an unkind word about anyone. She was always there to offer advice or a strong shoulder to lean on, always without judgment or criticism. She was truly an angel among them.

But in the spring of 1999, Kristin's life changed once again. Reno Air was getting ready to fold its wings due to a recent buyout by American Airlines. Many of the Reno Air employees would soon merge into the American Airlines' system on August 30, 1999, when the final transition was completed. But working for American was not what Kristin wanted. It was just too big. She liked the close family feeling that Reno Air had and wanted to be more than just a number in the computer. Kristin once again resorted to prayer in her time of need.

"Father, I know I haven't been very obedient to Your Word lately, but I am so grateful for all You continue to do in my life. I feel I am at a crossroad right now with the choice that has befallen me. I don't know which way to go or what I am supposed to be doing. So I put my faith and trust in You. Please guide me, Lord, and let my choices be Yours also. In Jesus' name I pray. Amen."

In April, Kristin applied for a flight attendant position with Alaska Airlines and, to her delight, was accepted immediately. After all these years, she could not believe that her prayers had finally been answered! Kristin truly believed that God had His hands on her future. She was absolutely certain that she was right where He wanted her to be.

On May 31, 1999, after five long weeks of flight attendant training, Kristin finally graduated from Alaska Airlines and moved to her new base in Seattle, Washington. Though leaving her husband behind for sometimes weeks at a time was heartbreaking, Kristin adapted surprisingly well to her new surroundings. She could not believe her good fortune. Not many people are blessed with a job they have longed for all their lives, and for eight glorious months, Kristin Mills would be allowed to live her dream!

Chapter Three

THURSDAY, JANUARY 27, 2000
SEATTLE, WASHINGTON

"Hey Piglet, it's me, Pooh. It's about one thirty, and I just walked in the door," Kristin said as she left her sister a message. "I'm on reserve this weekend again, and I don't know where I'm going yet, but I have to talk to you. I'm going out dancing with some friends tonight, but call me later, okay? Love you!" Pooh was a nickname that Dawn had given her little sister when she was still in diapers, and it stuck. As Kristin got a little older, she figured Dawn needed a nickname, too. Soon thereafter she came up with "Piglet," from the Disney movie *Winnie the Pooh*. Eventually Kristin had given nicknames to her entire family, as well as many of her friends.

After placing the phone on her nightstand, Kristin

sprawled out on her bed in her small rented room in Seattle.
She lay there for several minutes just thinking and feeling
so incredibly blessed. After nearly eight months of flying
for Alaska Airlines, it was still hard for her to believe that
she was really there. She had waited so long for her dream
to transpire. Some days she was just so overwhelmed with
emotions that she could hardly fathom the miracle of it all.

Kristin genuinely loved her job, even when she was
so tired she could hardly move, which lately was more often
than not. Being on reserve was hard on her physically as well
as emotionally. It was hard being away from her husband.
Sometimes the separation put a great strain on their
relationship, though they rarely had arguments. There was
just no time. Being based in Seattle and having a home in Las
Vegas didn't help the situation, but Dave knew how much the
job meant to his wife. He would never have denied her the
chance at her dream, but sometimes he just wanted her to be
home with him where she belonged.

Kristin came home as often as her schedule allowed,
but sometimes it was days or even weeks in between. She
tried to ignore the loneliness by hanging out with other flight
attendants that she had befriended, but it wasn't the same.

Being close to her sister and parents helped her not feel so alone.

Dawn, her family, and their parents all lived in the small town of Sequim, Washington, which was about an hour and a half away from Seattle by ferry. It wasn't always easy to see them either, but it was closer than Las Vegas, Kristin reminded herself. Her family had moved to Sequim from Las Vegas when Kristin first started her job at Alaska Airlines. Dave decided not to make the move because he didn't want to leave his construction job or his friends, which meant Kristin had to commute, but she really didn't mind.

Chapter Four

Saturday, January 29, 2000
Seattle / Tacoma
International Airport

Kristin spent most of her day on "airport standby" with several other reserve flight attendants from Alaska Airlines. This standby procedure wasn't always a favorite because after a few hours of being stuck in one place, the flight attendants usually got extremely bored and a bit antsy. But when Kristin was there it was a different story. To help pass the time, Kristin suggested that they push all the couches in the crew lounge together into a big circle. Then for the next several hours they all watched movies, ate popcorn and candy, and bonded as they laughed and enjoyed each other's company.

Although this was the first time that many of them

had met Kristin, she talked to each one of them as if she had known them all of her life. She listened intently to their problems, and even offered words of wisdom and encouragement when necessary. Everyone noticed how "the new girl" glowed with life and love for her new job and fellow co-workers.

As the hours passed, some of the flight attendants were called out to do a trip, but Kristin was not one of them. When her "standby" time was up, she drove home to finish out what she thought would be her last two days on reserve. When she arrived, there was a message from Dawn on her voice mail. Kristin called her back, but there was no answer. After leaving another message, she headed straight for the kitchen. "A girl's got to eat," she said to herself and smiled.

Around 7:30 that evening the phone rang. Kristin figured it was probably her sister, but it wasn't. It was Dave.

"Hey, hon. How's it going over there?" he asked.

"Really good, considering I just sat at the airport all day and never got called. But I did meet some really nice people who were on standby with me," Kristin said cheerfully, looking for the good instead of the bad, which didn't surprise her husband. They had been together since Kristin was 16, and she only got nicer with age. "We watched a movie and had a great time. A couple of them got called out, but so far I haven't heard anything. So how are the party plans coming along?" she asked. Dave was hosting a Super Bowl party at their home in Las Vegas the next day, and Kristin had hoped to be there.

"Everything's done. Now all I need is you. I sure hope they don't call you. It would be great if you could be here. But if not, I'll understand. I know you'll be here soon. When are you off reserve?"

"At midnight tomorrow night. Of course that all depends on whether I'm called, and how long of a trip they give me. I'm at their beck and call, but I really don't mind, though I wished I could be there, too, to help you with the party."

"Me too," he said sadly.

"So, what are you doing tonight?" Kristin asked him sweetly.

"Oh, I told my mom I'd stop by, but I wanted to talk to you first. So, I guess I should get going before it gets too late." Dave looked around their home, and then glanced down at the photograph of his wife on the end table. For a brief moment he wished that she were something other than a flight attendant, so they could be together more often. But the selfish thought didn't last. He knew she was doing exactly what she wanted, and that meant more to him than her being there. "I love you, Pooh. I'll see you soon, okay?"

"I love you, too. I'll try to call you when I know something. Have fun tomorrow if I don't make it back. Tell everyone I said hello." After they hung up, Kristin gave her sister another try, but there was still no answer.

As early Sunday approached, Kristin thought she might not have to go out at all since she still hadn't heard from scheduling. Normally she'd be looking forward to the trip, but this time she wanted to be home with her husband. But it was not meant to be. At the last minute one of her colleagues got sick. Crew Scheduling called her to pick up the trip. She had to be at the airport by 6:00 that morning.

Kristin left in such a hurry that there was no time for

her to make her bed, pick up her clothes, or even call her family to tell them where she was going.

Chapter Five
Sunday, January 30, 2000
Seattle, Washington
en route to Mexico

It was a cloudy, but beautiful winter morning in
Seattle, but Kristin didn't noticed. She was running late and
barely made it to the airport. Her trip on Flight 158 started in
Seattle and went to San Francisco, then on to Puerto Vallarta,
Mexico. It was a 24–hour layover, and Kristin really didn't
mind going. After all, it was winter! Who wouldn't want to go
to Puerto Vallarta, even if it was only for a day?

As she walked down the aircraft aisle to her station
in the back, Kristin suddenly remembered the promise
Dave made her the last time she did this trip. He told her he
would go to Mexico with her the next time that she went. But
even if time had allowed him to meet up with her, Dave still

wouldn't have been able to go. Not this time. He had to be in Las Vegas for their Super Bowl party.

"It's okay," she whispered, as she lowered herself into her jumpseat. "We'll have plenty of time to be together when I get home."

The two other flight attendants working the flight were Allison Shanks, the lead flight attendant working in First Class, and Craig Pulanco in the number three position seated at the tailcone exit. Both of them were based in Seattle.

Kristin was the number two flight attendant seated just inside the second galley in the main cabin on the left. She liked the number two position on the MD–83. It was the only position that gave her the opportunity to actually see the passengers' faces and talk to them during the flight while still in her jumpseat.

After all the passengers had boarded, Kristin sat in her seat and looked out the small porthole window on the right. She loved this part of her job, just before dawn when it was peaceful and quiet with nothing but the sound of the engines humming throughout the cabin. The sun was just beginning to crest the horizon, fighting its way through the clouds.

The engines roared, and the plane began to move quickly down the runway as it built up the momentum it needed for takeoff. She noticed how some of the passengers jumped with the slightest noise or bump. The seasoned travelers just sat back and enjoyed the trip.

Kristin was one of the few flight attendants that took it very personally when a passenger felt uncomfortable or afraid. She always went out of her way to assure him or her that everything was fine, and that the bumps and noises were perfectly normal. Flight attendants are trained to remain calm no matter what the situation, even during an unusually turbulent flight. On this particular flight, there were a few bumps across the water and some again after taking off from SFO, but nothing too extreme. Kristin was grateful that she had never really encountered anything serious since her career began in 1996 with Reno Air.

While scanning the immediate area, her gaze fell upon a family of four. Kristin couldn't help but smile. Their voices were full of excitement and anticipation as they looked out the window during their climb out of San Francisco toward their final destination: the sunny beaches of Puerto Vallarta!

That family made her think of her family. Kristin suddenly remembered that she hadn't talked to Dawn before she left. She made a mental note to call her again as soon as she returned.

The flight to Puerto Vallarta was routine and uneventful. Upon arrival at 1:23 in the afternoon local time, the crew was driven to the Westin Hotel on Puerto Vallarta's Harbor Beach. Kristin quickly changed her clothes and made a mad dash for the pool. She stayed there for several hours talking, laughing, and spreading cheer to anyone who would listen. For a passerby, it was hard not to notice the striking young beauty.

Several hours later Kristin glanced at her watch, then grabbed for her towel. It was just past 4:30, and she needed to get in the shower. Earlier she had made plans to join her crew for dinner, and she didn't want to keep them waiting.

As she made her way back to her room, she looked at her surroundings. Once again Kristin said a silent prayer of thanks for all she had, and all God continued to provide. Her life was so full. She had a wonderful family and husband, and the best job anyone could ever hope to have. She just couldn't thank God enough.

By the time Kristin met up with her co-workers, they were already in the lounge watching the last half of the Super Bowl game between the Tennessee Titans and the St. Louis Rams. The only one missing was Craig. He decided to have dinner with a friend.

When the game was over, the four of them sat there for several hours longer trying to learn all they could about one another, knowing it might be several months, or possibly years, before they ever flew together again. They talked about everything from families and hobbies to the jobs they had prior to Alaska Airlines.

"Before I came to work for Alaska in August 1982, I was flying cargo planes for eight years in the United States Air Force!" 53-year-old, Los Angeles-based Captain Ted Thompson told them.

"Well, I can do better than that! I spent 20 years of my life in the United States Navy flying transport aircraft before

Alaska hired me in July of 1985. I think I like this job much better," said 57–year–old First Officer Bill Tansky, who was also based in Los Angeles.

"Well, I can't beat either one of you, because I've only been with Alaska for eight months. In fact, it will be exactly eight months tomorrow! And prior to this job, I was with Reno Air for over two years before they were sold to American Airlines. So I guess you win, Bill, for lasting the longest in one place. But I bet you don't love doing this job more than I do. It's what I live for, except for my family and husband, of course," the twenty–six year old told her peers proudly.

"You are way too nice, Ms. Kristin Mills. Are you for real or what?" Ted teased, and they all laughed.

Just before midnight Kristin left the lounge and went to her room. She thought about calling Dave, but then decided against it. She wasn't sure what the time difference was, and she didn't want to wake him if he was already asleep. Besides, she knew she would see him soon. Maybe even sooner if her plan worked.

She didn't know exactly what time their flight was due to arrive in Seattle the next evening. But she hoped it was early enough so that she could catch the last flight out from there to Las Vegas. Dave wasn't expecting her, and normally Kristin would just wait until the next day to go home. But for some reason, she really missed her husband. She wanted to be home with him as soon as she could.

Kristin knew it would be a pleasant surprise for him, and one she would also enjoy. She made a mental note to check the flight schedule when they landed at SFO. Then she crawled into bed and fell asleep immediately.

The next morning Kristin woke refreshed and ready for the long journey home.

Chapter Six
MONDAY, JANUARY 31, 2000
GOING HOME

Early the next afternoon the flight crew met in the lobby, and together they rode to the airport. The weather was warm with mostly clear skies. At 1:37 p.m., 30 minutes later than scheduled, Alaska Airlines Flight 261 left Lic Gustavo Diaz Ordaz International Airport in Puerto Vallarta, Mexico, en route to Seattle/Tacoma International Airport in Seattle, Washington. An intermediate stop was planned at San Francisco International Airport in San Francisco, California.

The plane began to climb to its assigned cruising altitude of 31,000 feet. On board there were five crew members, 10 passengers in First Class, and 70 passengers scattered in the main cabin, along with three children under the age of two.

At 23,400 feet

The first sign of trouble started when the horizontal stabilizer jammed, although no one except the pilots were aware of the problem. The problem itself wasn't that unusual, and the pilots were confident at this point that they could handle the situation.

At 28,557 feet

The autopilot was disconnected. For the next seven minutes, the aircraft climbed at a much slower rate, because the pilots had to fly the plane manually. Nothing was said to the flight attendants, and their service went on as scheduled.

Kristin, Allison, and Craig sat in their assigned jumpseats and waited for the signal. A special color light and chime told them it was safe to get up and begin their in-flight service. Kristin was in the number two position again. She went to the back galley, where she immediately began preparing the carts for their lunch and beverage service. Craig, who was number three, was still in his seat talking to a nearby male passenger. When he noticed Kristin setting up the carts, he jumped up to assist her.

Up front in First Class, Allison was getting ready to start her service. She was once again the lead flight attendant. Kristin looked down the aisle just as Allison was closing the curtain, which separated the main cabin from the First Class section. They smiled at each other and they both waved. It never takes long to become good friends during a trip. Kristin felt she had made one with Allison.

After the carts were set up, Kristin and Craig rolled them to the front of the plane. They filled drink orders as they served the passengers their meals. Kristin made small talk to several of the passengers, trying as she always did to get to know something about each one before they all went their separate ways. As she reached row seven, her service was interrupted.

"Excuse me. Would you mind if we sat in the back?" the man asked curiously. "There are six of us, and it looks like there's a lot more room back there for us to relax and stretch out. We'd really appreciate it." The man had his wife and four small children with him. The youngest child was an infant.

"Oh, no problem," Kristin said cheerfully, making sure

the seatbelt sign was off. "It will be a few minutes before we get your order. But you can go back there now if you want." Kristin did her best to accommodate all of them. Several other passengers followed suit, taking advantage of the extra space.

Kristin soon discovered that most of the people on board were Alaska Airlines employees. There were several friends and family members from other airlines, as well. Craig had also brought along his good friend Paul, who was sitting in the back near the tailcone exit where Craig was stationed. Paul had flown over with them the day before, as did a few of the other non–revenue passengers.

Midway through their service Kristin came across Linda and Joe Knight. They were returning from a missionary trip in Mexico and were on their way back home to Monroe, Washington. She felt an immediate connection when she spoke to them. It was as if she had known them all her life.

She also had a chance to talk a little to the family of six who had just moved to the back of the plane. Their name was Clemetson, and they were also from Seattle. One of their children, Coriander, was seated directly across the aisle from her jumpseat. She handed the little girl her drink and smiled.

"When I get through with my service, maybe you can help me clean up a little. These people are quite messy!" Kristin joked as she winked at her new friend.

After her service was completed, Kristin gave Coriander a small bag and sent her through the cabin to pick up any leftover cups and napkins. Her young helper seemed happy to assist.

Kristin soon learned that both the Knight and Clemetson's families would be making the entire trip with her all the way back to Seattle. That meant plenty of time for her to visit with all of them. Their flight was due to arrive in San Francisco around 5:15 that evening.

Chapter Seven
CRUISING ALTITUDE
31,000 FEET

Kristin moved about the cabin with ease, confident and friendly as she spoke to many of the people on board. She knew from experience that this could possibly be the last time she saw any of them on her flights. She was determined to make a lasting impression on them all.

"Can I get you another drink? Or maybe even another meal, if you really want to live dangerously!" Kristin laughed, knowing how some people felt about airline food. "We have some extra ones in the back if you're interested."

"Oh, no thank you, young lady, although it wasn't really that bad. I had a big breakfast this morning. I don't think I could eat another bite. But I will take another cookie for later, if you have one," said the man in 10–A.

Kristin walked back to the galley and returned with the man's cookie, and another soda to wash it down.

"Thank you so much. You know, this is the best flight I think I've ever had with your airline," he told her.

"Well, thank you, what a sweet thing to say. I'll be back to check on you. Would you like a blanket or pillow before I leave?"

"Sure, that would be great. Thanks."

After Kristin fulfilled his request, she went to the next person, and then the next, and the next. For nearly two hours, Kristin went up and down the aisle making her presence known. There wasn't one passenger to whom she didn't at least say hello.

Little did anyone know that up front in the cockpit, the pilots were trying to resolve, on their own, what they thought was a minor malfunction. The small wing on the back of the tail, known as the horizontal stabilizer, was giving them quite a challenge, and they weren't sure what to do. They wrestled with the controls for over an hour trying to keep the plane from nosing downward. They tried troubleshooting the problem themselves, until they had no other choice but to radio for assistance.

Kristin continued her mission to converse with any and all passengers who were still awake. She was at their disposal for whatever she could do for them. She purposely saved Joe and Linda Knight for last. She knew she would relate to them even before she knew what kind of work they did. They just seemed so kindhearted, so approachable, and incredibly sincere.

Kristin and the Knights talked for over half an hour. The couple shared with her their life as pastors in Monroe, Washington, which is about 45 minutes northeast of Seattle. They also talked of their yearly mission to Mexico.

"We've been doing this ministry for the past two years, going to the outskirts of Puerto Vallarta at the dump where many of the poorest families live. It is so sad to see these people going through the garbage for cans, bottles and even scraps of food, while living daily in unimaginable squalor and stench. And only a few short miles from one of the most famous resorts in all of Mexico!" Linda told Kristin through her tears, as she relived their visit.

"It's pretty much a forgotten part of the city, and totally ignored by the government," her husband added. "The only way these people can survive is through volunteers and donations. It really touches your heart to see the children there. And it breaks my heart to see them suffer like they do. I want to do so much more."

In the two years that the Knights had been going to Mexico, they had raised over $50,000 through their 500–member congregation from The Rock Church in Monroe. It was enough money to help feed and clothe about 100 families living near the dump.

"We're going to go back there in March," Linda said excitedly. "With the funds we've received, we want to build a school and a community center near the dump. What a difference it will make in these people's lives. It will be something they can be proud of someday, too."

Kristin was moved by the couple's generosity and

enthusiasm for their project, and how much they seemed to enjoy their work as missionaries, and as pastors.

"God must be very proud of both of you," she told them. "I admire you for all your hard work and your courage to go back there to make right something that is very wrong. I don't know how you do it. But I know that we all have our gifts and talents that God wants us to use for His purpose. It's obvious that you have found yours. I haven't been very obedient to His Word lately. I'm just too easily swayed into the secular world, I guess, and I am not very proud of myself. But I still want to know what His plan is for me. Hopefully I will be ready and willing to hear what it is when He calls. But in the meantime, I will serve my people here to the best of my knowledge and skills, and pray that God doesn't give up on me," Kristin said sweetly.

"Don't ever think that, honey. God will never let Satan have his way with one of His children. You just keep asking for His mercy and forgiveness whenever you pray, and He will do the rest, I promise," Linda assured her.

"Thank you. I needed to hear that. Now could you call my mom and tell her?" she joked. Kristin hugged them both before she left. Then she made her way to the front to see if Allison needed any help in First Class.

When she got to the galley, Kristin saw her fellow co–worker sitting on her jumpseat reading a *People* magazine that was left on board. It was obvious that her assistance was not needed. Allison looked up and caught the eye of her new young friend, and smiled. Kristin smiled back, and Allison resumed her reading.

Kristin headed toward the back of the plane, picking up garbage along the way. Many of the passengers were napping, and a few others asked her for refills on their beverages. When Kristin reached her station, she heard the call.

Three chimes and a red light told her it wasn't good. She took the phone from its cradle and listened, as Captain Ted Thompson gave Allison the news.

"I'm going to need you to clean up the cabin, and secure all the carts and luggage. Then you will all need to get in your seats until I get back to you. We've been having a little trouble with the stabilizer, and we may have to put her down at LAX. So, secure the cabin, and I'll keep you informed," Ted told her. With his nearly thirty years of flying experience, Ted felt he and his First Officer, Bill Tansky, could handle the problem. He didn't want to alarm his crew unnecessarily, but he wanted the cabin and his flight attendants secure, just to be safe.

"Do you know how much time we have to get everything put away?" the lead flight attendant asked calmly.

"It's hard to say at this point, Allison. Just do it as quickly as you can," the Captain replied.

"Do you want me to make an announcement or will you?" Allison was following procedure and needed to know.

"I will. You and the others just get everything picked up. And make sure it's secure! There's a chance it could get pretty bumpy. You'll probably need to do an emergency demo just as a precaution. After you're done, get in your seats and strap yourselves in. I'll call you back when I can and update you on any information we get."

After they hung up, Allison continued to follow

emergency training procedure, ringing three times to get the attention of her co-workers. It was the most crucial of all warnings, hearing the three chimes, which immediately let the other flight attendants know of the impending danger ahead.

"I'm here, Allison," Kristin said, "and I heard everything. I'll pass the Captain's instructions along to Craig. Let me know if you need me to help you up there."

Kristin wasn't sure what she should be feeling at this point, but fear was trying its best to surface. She knew that being afraid was not God's will for anyone. It was like telling Him that you don't trust Him. She knew, too, that fear gave Satan more power over situations that he normally couldn't control. Kristin refused to let that happen.

As she walked down the narrow aisle of the plane, the wisdom of her mother's words a few weeks earlier filled her mind and grabbed her heart. "Are you ready to go?" her mother had asked when Kristin was afraid to get on that small plane. Two weeks ago Kristin couldn't honestly say whether she was ready or not. "Am I ready now?" she asked herself, trying her best to ignore the mounting fear inside.

There was no time to waste.

Kristin quickened her pace as she walked toward the galley. Then closing the curtain she dropped to her knees in desperate prayer.

"Lord, I need You. Please lift this fear from my heart and give me Your strength. I know I have fallen away from You for so many years. What a fool I have been! Please forgive me. If it is Your time and will for me to go today, then please help me to be ready for the journey. And, Lord, let me help You to ready the others here too, so that they will know there is a better place for all of us. Use me, Lord. I am here for You. In Your Son's precious name I pray. Amen." When she finished, the fear that tried to overtake her emotions earlier had all but vanished. Kristin left the galley and quickly joined the others.

Though somewhat anxious, the flight attendants acted completely professional, doing everything they were supposed to do, in a timely fashion. Their years of training kicked in. Together they quickly and thoroughly cleaned the cabin, stowing all the carts, taking away half–full drinks and a few uneaten meals and throwing them into the garbage.

As they cleaned and stowed, the Captain's voice came across loud and clear throughout the cabin.

"Ladies and gentlemen, I am going to turn on the seatbelt sign for a bit. We are experiencing some minor problems up here, and though I am confident at this point that it isn't anything to be alarmed about, we need you to stay in your seats just to be safe. We will need your full cooperation in getting your luggage stowed in the overhead bins or underneath the seat in front of you. The flight attendants are going to come around and make sure everything is secure. Then they will show you a quick demo on where your closest exits are and how your life vest works, just in case you forgot. I remind you again that this is just a precaution. When they are through, I have asked them to stay in their seats until further notice. Thank you all for listening. Please remain in your seats as well, with your seatbelts fastened low and tight until the seatbelt sign has been turned off."

The flight attendants retrieved their demo equipment. Then they got into position. Allison talked while Kristin stood near the bulkhead. Craig was in the main cabin near the over–wing exits.

They all demonstrated once again, in more detail, where their closest exits were located, how their life vest worked, and that their blue–and–gray seat cushion could also be used as a floatation device, if necessary. Kristin's heart was racing. She noticed, too, that Allison was talking a little faster than normal, but no one else did.

The cabin grew silent. The passengers watched closely as the trio performed their duties, looking for any sign of doubt or fear on their faces. But the crew stayed calm and focused.

When they finished, the attendants quickly returned to their seats. As soon as they sat down and strapped themselves in, a loud bang was heard near the back of the plane. The sound echoed throughout the cabin. Suddenly the plane began losing altitude, plunging nose–first toward the earth below.

Chapter Eight
STABLE AT 23,500 FEET

4:10 P.M.

The aircraft nose–dived from 31,000 feet to 26,000
feet. Then within seconds, it fell again at an incredible
and unbelievable rate of 1,000 feet per second to 23,500
feet, throwing around anything and everything that wasn't
strapped down. It was as if a dozen tornadoes had blown
through the cabin all at one time. Many of the overhead
compartments had been jarred open from the force. Their
contents ended up several rows in front or behind where
they had originated, and debris was strewn everywhere.
Though the cabin did not suffer from decompression, several
oxygen masks had come loose and were dangling above the
passengers' heads.

From her jumpseat, Kristin saw the unbelievable chaos and havoc left behind by their sudden and unexpected tumble. The passengers were still in their seats, though they were frightened out of their minds. But at least they were all alive, from what she could tell. Their screams had died down, as if preparing themselves for whatever was coming next.

The people in the back of the plane looked to Kristin and Craig for reassurance and comfort. Though her heart was pounding against her chest, Kristin did not hesitate for a moment as she grabbed for the phone.

"Ladies and gentlemen, please remain in your seats until the seatbelt sign has been turned off. I can assure you that Captain Thompson and First Officer Tansky have everything under control. They are doing their best to land us safely, but they will need your full cooperation. If there is anyone that needs immediate assistance, please ring your passenger call button above your head, and one of us will come to you shortly. The rest of you please stay where you are. We will be with you as soon as possible," Kristin managed to say with more strength and confidence than she ever knew she had.

Several of the passengers rang their call button, but miraculously there were only a few minor injuries. One passenger needed a large Band–Aid on his forearm from a cut he received from a flying briefcase. A young girl had scraped her chin on the armrest. One of the older passengers was short of breath and needed to be put on oxygen. Everyone was amazed that no one was seriously hurt in the fall. But there was an unbelievable mess everywhere. Personal items, portable disc players, cell phones, baby bottles, and purses were scattered from the front of the aircraft all the way to the back.

Then came the voice they had all been waiting for.

"Folks, we have had a flight control problem up front here, and we are working on it," Ted Thompson told them. "That's Los Angeles off to the right and that's where we're headed. We're pretty busy up here working this situation, but I don't anticipate any big problems. We'll be going to LAX, and I'd anticipate us parking there in about twenty to thirty minutes. Please remain in your seats with your seatbelts fastened for the duration of the flight. We apologize for the bumpy ride and for any inconvenience."

The flight attendants tried to clean up and attend to the most needy first. The rest of the passengers looked on in disbelief. Suddenly, there was another incredibly loud bang followed by a much louder popping. It was obvious to everyone that these weren't normal airplane sounds.

Once again the noises were centered toward the back of the plane. Allison had just come out of First Class to help the other crewmembers when she heard it too. They all looked at each other and wondered what was coming next.

Allison immediately turned and headed for the cockpit. Just as she reached for the door, it opened.

"I was just coming up," she said to the Captain, noticing the disarray of papers scattered everywhere.

"I need everything picked up, and everybody strapped down! I'm gonna unload the airplane and see if we can regain control of it," Ted Thompson announced.

"Okay. I thought you should know that we just heard another big bang back there," Allison told him.

"Yeah, I heard it. It's the stabilizer trim, I think. You guys heard it too?"

"Yeah, and it was really loud," she confirmed. "By the way, Kristin already did an announcement before you did. She told them to stay in their seats. I don't think they'll be going anywhere. I'll tell the others to make sure that everything is secure."

Allison left the cockpit and closed the door behind her. She immediately called Kristin and Craig.

"Ted said we need to clean up and sit down. I'm okay up here. Let me know when you're both safely in your seats."

"Okay. Hey, Allison, are you really okay? I mean really?" Kristin asked with great concern.

"I won't tell you that I'm not scared, because I am," she told her colleague honestly. "But I know we'll be all right just as soon as we get on the ground. But Kristin, could you do us all a favor? You seem to have a special connection with the Man upstairs, so do you think you could say a prayer for us? Maybe when you get back in your jumpseat, you could let

Him know that we could sure use His help!"

"I already did. But it never hurts to say another one. And you can be sure that God has His hands on all of us right now, and He will keep them there until we're safely home. It will be okay, I promise. I'll talk to you when we get on the ground. God bless you, Allison. Keep the faith."

Kristin didn't know what would happen next. No one did. But no matter what they had to endure, for whatever reasons they had to endure them, she did her best to remain confident. She knew God would guide her to do and say whatever was necessary to comfort these people in their time of need.

As she walked back to her station, Kristin wondered if this could be her calling. "Is this Your plan and purpose for me to be here with all of these people, Lord?" she asked silently. "If so, please help me to be ready for whatever it is You need me to do."

When she reached her seat all eyes were on her. Their panic was obvious. They were searching for answers and wanted to be assured that everything was going to be okay.

Kristin smiled that incredibly beautiful and very contagious smile. Then with more confidence and certainty than she had ever known before, she told them what she truly believed.

"Don't worry. Everything is going to be just fine," she announced to the small group in the back. "Our pilots are the best and they will do everything they can to get us on the ground safely. We should be landing very shortly."

Her words seemed to calm everyone, at least temporarily. Just as she strapped herself into her jumpseat, Kristin noticed the little Clemetson girl across the aisle. Coriander had her hands over her face. Her little shoulders shook up and down, though she was trying hard not to cry. Immediately Kristin undid her seatbelt and grabbed the phone from its cradle. Then, breaking all the rules, she left her station and got into Coriander's seat with her. She placed the child on her lap and wrapped the seatbelt low and tight around them both. Then Kristin began doing what she felt God was calling her to do. Her prayer was heard throughout the plane.

"Father, please help us," Kristin said over the noise of

the engines. "So many of us here have ignored You through the years, myself included. Now that we need You most, Lord, we come humbly to our knees. We know we don't deserve it, but we ask for Your mercy on us all. We're in trouble, Father. Give us Your strength to get us through. Please guide us to safety. Help all of us know that You are the true Pilot of our lives. You are the only One that can save us. Not only from this disaster, if it is Your will, but also from the depths of hell. Please help these new friends of mine know who Jesus is and understand what He did for us on the cross. Please help them to know that He died for all of us, to rid us of our sins, in order for us to someday live with You for eternity. Forgive us for not knowing You sooner or following You better…"

Just as her prayer had ended the plane began spinning, tumbling, spiraling, and corkscrewing, as it fell from the sky, flying upside down for several minutes at a time.

Trying her best to protect Coriander, Kristin bent forward as far as she could go. She held the little girl tight, as their bodies were tossed back and forth like rag dolls.

"It's okay, honey. Don't worry, everything will be okay, I promise," she whispered into the whimpering child's ear.

But the fear was mounting inside of Kristin, and this time it wouldn't go away.

"Oh, Dear God, I don't want to die," she said under her breath, so no one would hear. "There's so much more I want to do with my life. I've messed it up so badly. Don't take it away, Lord, not yet. Let me make it right first. Let me show You that I can be what You want and need me to be, please?" she begged.

As these thoughts crossed her mind, so, too, did the words of Jesus when He prayed in the Garden of Gethsemane that if it were possible, the hour might pass from Him too. "Abba, Father, all things are possible for You. Take this cup away from Me; nevertheless, not what I will, but what You will" (Mark 14:36).

Jesus didn't want to die that way, hanging on a cross, beaten, whipped and torn to shreds, but He knew He had to. It was God's plan. At that moment, Kristin knew for certain that something terrible was about to happen to her, too.

As the screams and mayhem continued, unbelievable destruction raced through the cabin with incredible force.

Then without warning, it stopped. And for a brief few seconds, no one moved or made a sound.

The plane was shaky, but stable. Kristin looked up cautiously. For a few moments she thought the disaster had ended. She glanced over toward the window. There she saw the most magnificent sunset. It was only in the beginning stages and was already too beautiful for words. Kristin wondered if the others had seen it too. It was as if God was giving them all a preview of what heaven would be like.

Then as quickly as the chaos stopped, it started again. The plane spiraled downward once more, but with much greater force than before…never stalling, never slowing, never stopping. Suddenly, there was a voice from out of nowhere, yet it seemed to be everywhere.

"Fear not, for I have redeemed you; I have called you by your name; You are Mine."

She recognized the verse from Isaiah 43:1 immediately. Kristin wasn't sure if everyone heard it, but she knew without a doubt whose voice it was. And with His words came an unexplainable peace deep down inside of her.

At last, Kristin finally understood. It had been God's plan all along for her to be on this flight. From the very beginning, she was meant to help these people through their last and worst earthly tragedy and to lead them to Him. The invitation was there for everyone, but only if they chose to hear it. Kristin knew there wasn't anyone that God won't use to bring Him glory. And to her surprise and very humble heart, she felt blessed that He had chosen her.

Kristin sat there watching all the turmoil as the plane jerked, tumbled, and fell, but strangely, she was no longer afraid. Holding Coriander tightly, her thoughts suddenly went to Dave. She wished she had called him last night like she wanted. They had been through so much in ten years, and through it all he was still her best friend.

"Take care of him for me, Lord. Dry his tears, and let him find happiness again soon," she prayed silently.

Then for the last time, Kristin thought about her sister, Dawn, and her mother and father. She loved them so much. She asked God to take care of them too, and to ease their pain, letting them remember her with love and kindness forever, until they meet again. "And please, Lord, somehow let them all know that I was finally ready to go."

Her final words came from the 23rd Psalm, as Kristin recited the familiar Scripture that she had learned as a child. She felt it fitting to share with her new "family" on board to help comfort them through this final disaster. She knew, too, that the Knights were doing their part, telling those who sat near them of God's amazing grace and love and the sacrifice Jesus made for everyone. She felt incredibly blessed that they were on this flight with her.

The screaming around Kristin ceased with her first few words.

"The Lord is my shepherd. I shall not want. He makes me to lie down in green pastures; He leads me beside the still waters. Yea, though I walk through the valley of the shadow of death, I will fear no evil; For You are with me... Jesus, please come into our hearts and forgive us for what we have done in this life. Let us know You now, Lord, as our Redeemer and Savior. Take us home with You, Father," Kristin prayed out loud.

From the window she saw the water's edge and knew

it was almost over. Kristin grabbed Coriander firmly against her chest. Then she closed her eyes.

Chapter Nine
FROM THE COCKPIT

The warning system inside the cockpit was on overload. A cacophony of alarms screamed at the pilots as they continued their struggle, but there was nothing more they could do.

"Mayday, Mayday," Bill Tansky hollered into the radio, but no one heard his words. The flight crew had no idea that they had been disconnected from the world below.

"Push and roll, push and roll. We're inverted. Push, push, the blue side up," Ted yelled to his First Officer, desperately trying to find the blue of the sky once again. "We need to be blue side up, Bill!"

"I'm pushing, Ted."

"Okay, now let's kick the rudder. Left rudder, left rudder…"

"I can't reach it," Bill screamed back, as his pulse raced faster than ever.

"Okay then, right rudder. Right rudder. Are we flying? Yeah, we're flying. Tell them what we're doing. We got to get it over, but at least upside down we're flying," the Captain cried out, trying hard to regain control of the 80–ton jet.

The pilots were tired, nauseous, and disoriented as the plane turned and rolled from side to side, but they hung on with all their strength.

Another loud noise was heard throughout the doomed airliner, then another and another. Finally the massive wounded bird of steel gave up the fight, plunging quickly toward the earth below.

Seconds before 4:21 p.m. Pacific Standard Time, Alaska Airlines Flight 261 was seen flying upside down, before it plummeted nose–first into the 58–degree waters of the Pacific Ocean off the coast of Los Angeles, about 2.7

miles north of Anacapa Island, California.

"Ah, here we go," were the last words heard from the cockpit that day. Then there was silence.

At 4:26 p.m. Alaska Airlines Flight 261 was reported down.

Chapter Ten

Monday, January 31, 2000
Sequim, Washington

Dawn Germain was wandering around Port Townsend shopping with her husband, Larry, their son, Daniel, and his friend. At 4:45 that afternoon, a lady came rushing into the store where Dawn was browsing. She told the clerk that there had been a plane crash off the coast of Los Angeles.

Dawn had overheard the conversation and immediately began asking questions.

"I don't mean to eavesdrop, but did they say what airline it was?" she asked the lady.

"They didn't give out too many details," the woman

said, "but they did confirm that it was an Alaska Airlines' plane. I think they said it came from somewhere in Mexico."

Dawn reached in her purse for her cell phone. She needed to call her mom to see if she knew anything about the accident. When she went to dial the number, she noticed that her mom had already been trying to call.

"Mom, have you heard from Kristin?" she asked anxiously. Her mother had answered on the first ring.

"Dawn, where have you been?" Relief rushed through Leslie Batdorf as she heard her daughter's voice. "Did you hear about the crash? It was Alaska Airlines. It just can't be Kristin. We haven't been able to get a hold of her, and no one knows where she was supposed to be going! Your dad called the 800 number that he saw on the news, but we still don't know anything yet," she whimpered, trying hard not to think the worst.

"Calm down, Mom. Have you heard from Dave? Maybe he knows something," Dawn replied.

"We tried calling, but he didn't answer."

"I'll call him. We're just leaving Port Townsend. We'll be home in less than thirty minutes. Call me on my cell if you hear anything. And Mom, try not to worry. Kristin will be fine, I promise," Dawn assured her, though she had a hard time believing it herself.

As they drove home, Dawn said a silent prayer hoping that God was listening.

"Oh, please let her be okay. Let her be safe. Just give me a sign, Lord. Give me a peace inside so I know for sure that she is okay. She's my best friend. I need her. Oh, God, I don't even remember what her favorite color is. What is it, baby blue? Oh why can't I remember? Please, God! I promise, if she's okay, I will ask her everything there is to know about her. Just let her be safe. Give me a sign. Make me feel the peace inside, please!" she begged. But peace never came.

Dawn called her mother again as soon as she got home to see if there was any news. Then she called Dave in Las Vegas, but he didn't know anything either. In a desperate attempt, she had even called her sister's cell phone and left her a message. But it went unheard.

Gene Batdorf put a call into Kristin's Seattle roommate, Tina Cooper, hoping that she might know his daughter's whereabouts.

"Do you have any idea where Kristin was going?" he asked her.

"All I know is that she was going to Mexico and that she was due home today. But I don't know any of the times or flight numbers. Oh God, you don't think it was her plane, do you, Mr. Batdorf?" Tina sobbed into the phone.

"We don't know yet, Tina. But I pray that it isn't. I have to make some phone calls. I'll let you know when we hear something."

For the next two hours, Kristin's family and friends prayed and waited. Around 7:30 that evening, Dawn's cell phone rang. It was the call that confirmed their worst fears.

"Dawn, this is Colleen from Alaska Airlines. Do you have someone with you right now?" she asked with great concern. Colleen was the Analyst Inflight Administrator for Alaska Airlines in charge of Crisis Response for Flight 261.

"Well, yes, I do. My husband is here. So is my son," Dawn said a bit confused. "Why do you ask?"

"I hate to have to tell you this, but your sister was one of the flight attendants on Flight 261. I can't tell you how deeply sorry we are. Our hearts and prayers go out to all of you." For a brief few seconds, no one spoke.

"Okay, wait a minute. I need to make sure I heard what you're saying. So you're telling me it was Kristin's plane. Is that right? There's no doubt in your mind?" Dawn wanted to make sure she had heard it correctly.

"Yes, I'm so sorry," Colleen said.

"Oh dear, God, no. It just can't be."

Immediately Colleen started giving Dawn phone numbers to call, just in case she needed any help after it all sunk in. Dawn was frantically trying to write the numbers down, but she had no idea why. Colleen had also asked for her parents' and Dave's phone numbers.

Eleven–year–old Daniel Germain was sitting in the living room when he heard his mother talking and confirming that his aunt was on the plane.

"No! No!" he screamed and ran to his bedroom, slamming the door behind him.

When Dawn hung up, all of her thoughts went to Kristin. No more could she pretend that everything would be all right. The firm bite of reality grabbed her hard. She fell to her knees and began crying hysterically. Her husband, Larry, was there within seconds, lifting her up and holding her close to him.

"Not Kristin. Oh, God, no, Larry. Why would He do this? How could God let this happen?" she sobbed into her husband's shirt.

"I don't know, honey. I just don't know. But we have to stay strong. We still need to tell your mom and dad. Do you want to call, or should we just go over there?" he asked.

"We have to go there. Get Daniel. He's in his room. I'll get our coats." Dawn clung to what seemed to be her last ounce of strength, though she had no idea where it came from. She hoped it would last long enough for her to break the tragic news to her parents.

When they arrived, Leslie met them at the door. Gene was on the phone with his sister in the kitchen. But Dawn and Larry assumed that he was talking to Colleen from Alaska Airlines, which meant they already heard the news.

"So you know," Dawn said matter–of–factly, looking over at her dad.

"Know what?" her mother asked somewhat confused.

"That it was Kristin's plane. Isn't dad talking to them?"

"No!" her mother screamed. "No, not Kristin. Not my baby! Oh please, Dear God, no!" Without any warning, Leslie's legs buckled beneath her and she fell to the floor in a heap, as she grabbed the sides of her head in disbelief. The pain burned through her like a wild fire out of control.

Gene dropped the phone and was at her side immediately. He held his wife close and rocked her in his arms like a child, as tears flooded his cheeks. The pain sunk in, and his heart cried out in anguish prayer.

"Help us, Lord. Please, help us," he whimpered like a wounded animal.

Wrapped in sorrow and overcome with grief, his thoughts suddenly went to Psalm 73:26. "My flesh and my heart may fail; but God is the strength of my heart and my portion forever." Just as the words came to him, Gene was overwhelmed by a strong sense of comfort. It was as if God were right there on the floor holding him, willing His strength into Gene's newly shattered heart. Gene knew he had to remain strong for his family.

"Thank you, Father. We know we can't do anything without You. But this test will surely be our biggest challenge and the worst heartache of all. Please stay with us and provide us all with the strength and courage we will need to get through these next few weeks and months. In Jesus' name, I pray. Amen."

Gene knew it was only the beginning of a very painful journey for him and his family, but he trusted God with everything, even the reasoning behind the tragic loss of his youngest child.

As her parents continued to console one another, Dawn called Dave. When he answered, she had to be the bearer of bad news once again. But he didn't believe it.

"No way! I just talked to someone over there. They told me that Kristin wasn't on that plane! You have to be mistaken, Dawn. It wasn't her!"

Dave had also been calling the 800 number for several hours. At first they couldn't find any record of Kristin being on board, and they told him so. But they were the ones who had been gravely mistaken. Another call came in just seconds after hanging up from Dawn, confirming the most unimaginable nightmare he had ever known.

"It can't be. She can't be gone," he screamed out loud. Dave reached over and grabbed his wife's picture from the end table. He held it as close to his heart as he could get it. "Help me, God. If this is Your will, please, help me to understand it!" he begged.

Dave felt himself sinking into a dark unknown abyss, surrounded by such sadness that, until that day, he never knew existed.

3:00 a.m.

Dawn paced the floor. She couldn't sleep. She could barely think. She was still numb from the news she had heard earlier that day. Dawn knew she would be for a very long time. Her little sister was gone. How could this happen? How could God take such an incredibly wonderful girl, and in such a horrific way? What did Kristin ever do to deserve it? What did any of us do? She asked silently, as she fell to her knees in prayer.

"God, please help me! I just don't understand any of this," she whispered softly. "I would never attempt to question Your plan, Lord, if I could only make sense of it. The pain right now is just so overwhelming. I need to hear Your voice. Tell me why it had to be Kristin? If this was Your purpose for her, then show me what good will come from it! Help me to understand. Please, Lord. I need to know."

Chapter Eleven

Monday, January 31, 2000
The Last Sunset
Southern California

The sun had just begun to descend over the southern California coastline. For nearly a week the rain and cloud cover had plagued all the cities in the area, leaving behind a gloomy, damp, and somewhat depressive mood. Then suddenly, without warning, the sun burst through the thick gray covering, bringing into view the most awesome sight.

As the big yellow ball dropped below the horizon, unusually bright and intense colors filled the once dreary skies. The sunset-of-all-sunsets started to form. Never before had anyone seen such an incredible array of colors. A yellow bank of clouds settled under different shades of purples, pinks, blues, and oranges, forming billows of fluffy clouds that were scattered all across the sky. It was truly breathtaking!

People along the coast went outside to experience the awesome event. Flash bulbs were going off in all directions as onlookers tried to capture the inexplicable beauty of the evening sky. No one had yet heard about the airplane that crashed a few miles off shore only a half an hour earlier.

When the pictures were developed a couple of days later, it was hard not to notice the distinct image suspended high above the skyline. It was the image of an angel with long flowing hair and large wings. It seemed obvious why she was there. She had come to earth to help. She, too, was doing God's work in that final moment before Alaska Airlines' Flight 261 fell from the sky.

The picture was shared in many local newspapers and all across the Internet. It proved to be a great comfort for many families of the victims on board, helping them to better cope with their loss.

Chapter Twelve
THURSDAY, FEBRUARY 10, 2000
GRIEVING HEARTS

Kristin's memorial service was held in Las Vegas, Nevada, on February 10, 2000, at the Shadow Hills Baptist Church on Vegas Drive. More than 400 people attended the service. The long list included family members, friends, co–workers, and fellow flight attendants from Reno Air, American Airlines, and Alaska Airlines, as well as from several other major airlines. They wanted to pay their last respects to one of their own, the girl they found so incredibly charming and so very easy to love.

Many of Kristin's friends were asked to say a few words, and many of them did. But the more they talked, the more they cried. Then Dave read a letter he wrote to his wife shortly after the crash. He wanted to share it with her family and friends, just in case Kristin was close enough to hear.

To My Wife, Kristin:

You were my best friend. You were the kind of person one only meets once in a lifetime. When you walked into a room, you couldn't help but be noticed. Your spirit was free, and you lived life to its fullest. Your smile always lifted me when I had a bad day. And sometimes when I was frustrated with life, you always said something silly and made me laugh until I forgot why I was upset.

You didn't take things too seriously, except your job. For as long as I knew you, there was only one job you ever dreamed of doing. Besides dancing, you always wanted to be a flight attendant and work for Alaska Airlines. When the opportunity was presented, you went full out to accomplish your dream. You were never a quitter, even when it was hard to be away from your family and from me for many days at a time. You stayed so focused and so strong.

One of your best qualities was that you had the ability to make a complete stranger smile and feel important. You never judged anyone by their appearance or their flaws. You only focused on the good in people.

It gives me great comfort just knowing you died doing exactly what you loved to do. I know in my heart in those final moments when the plane was going down that you were not just working for Alaska Airlines preparing everyone for an emergency like you were taught. You were also working for God, in comforting those who were frightened. Your heart was immeasurable.

I was blessed to have spent ten years of my life with you. They were the best years of my life. I know that you will be with me in spirit for the rest of my life. I know, too, that one day I will see you again in heaven, and that you will once again make me laugh. And we will be together again, forever.

I will never forget you, Kristin. And I will never stop loving you until the day I die.

For several weeks following the service, Dave had a constant stream of people coming in and out of his home, bringing him food and trying hard to console him. For this he was very thankful. It helped him feel not quite so alone. It was almost as if he could pretend that Kristin was on one of her trips and would soon be returning home.

But after a while, the constant stream of mourners slowed to a trickle. After a few months, it stopped altogether. It was almost as if his wife had died all over again.

Dave was truly grateful to his in-laws, who seemed genuinely concerned for his well-being. Dawn called him every other day to see how he was holding up. Gene and Leslie called at least once a week, as well. Also, Aimee Harvey, with whom Kristin had roomed for five weeks during her training at Alaska, called several times a week just to check on him. Aimee still worked for Alaska Airlines. She first met Dave at Kristin's memorial service. Separately, their loss proved to be unbearable. But together Dave and Aimee drew strength and hope. Over the next several months, they became each other's support.

Chapter Thirteen
Message in a Bottle
Friday, March 3, 2000
Oxnard, California

"God, it hurts so much. Please, make it stop!" Dave cried out from his bed. It had been over a month since the plane crash, and he still couldn't believe that Kristin was gone. "What do I do now, Lord? Where do I go? How will I ever make it without her? Please help me!"

Dave had a hard time making sense of anything. His loneliness was, at times, too much to bear. He knew he needed to get away. He wondered if going to the crash site might help his troubled heart accept his loss better. Maybe it would even help him feel closer to Kristin.

One afternoon Dave jumped into his wife's little

Toyota and drove to southern California, where he checked into a room at the Embassy Suites Resort in Oxnard. That night he bought himself the most expensive bottle of Merlot he could find at a small convenience store nearby. Then he walked the few short steps down to the beach. The sun was just beginning to set. As he sat there all alone drinking his wine, his thoughts went to Kristin. He missed her so much. His emptiness was insufferable. He could hardly stand the pain.

With pen in hand, Dave began writing her another letter. Unlike the one from her memorial service, this letter was filled with memories of days gone by. With each word, his mind went back to the many years before, when they were together and so very happy. He could barely remember a life without her.

Tears filled his eyes and blurred his vision, but he kept writing. He wrote for what seemed like hours, until he had filled five pages full of precious memories and the bottle of wine was empty.

Dave rolled up the letter and put it in the bottle. Then he sealed it with the cork, and threw it into the ocean.

He knew Kristin would never see it, but it made him feel better just to have written his thoughts on paper. For several minutes he watched, as the waves rolled the bottle over and over, then slowly took it out to sea.

When it finally disappeared, Dave went to his room alone. There he dreamed, once again, of his beautiful wife and the life they had shared together. He wondered if he would ever find that kind of love again.

Chapter Fourteen
Wednesday, January 31, 2001
One Year Later

The victims' families and friends all met at Point Mugu Naval Air Station. From this area they could actually see where the plane had gone into the water, 11 miles out from the shoreline. The Navy Department gave special clearance for everyone to be brought in by buses. Dave, Dawn and her family, and her parents, along with hundreds of other people were going to spend the day remembering. A large tent was put up on the beach to accommodate everyone during the ceremony that was planned for later that afternoon.

Also on the beach that day was a vault. It was specially designed to hold any cards or letters from anyone who wanted to write one last message to his or her loved one.

As soon as all the letters were inside, the vault would be permanently sealed and dropped into the ocean. The Coast Guard planned to take it out the next morning to the exact location where the plane had gone down.

Before the ceremony started, Dawn met with Dave in the hotel lobby.

"How are you holding up?" she asked her brother-in-law with much concern. Dawn hadn't seen Dave in several months, and it looked as though he had lost some weight.

"Oh, it gets a little easier each day. But it still hurts," he replied. "How about you, Dawn? Are you doing okay?" He touched her arm and looked deep into her eyes. Dave knew that she was struggling, probably more than any of them.

"I'm okay, I guess. There are days when I think I'm fine. Then there are those really long days that I don't even want to get out of bed. I miss her, Dave," Dawn told him sadly. "I didn't just lose one person, you know? I lost three. She was my sister, but I helped raise her, too, so she was like my child. Then when she got older, she became my very best friend! It still hurts so much."

"I know. But it will get better. It has to. Praying helps me a lot. I've said so many prayers over the last year. I asked God to please just give me a sign, so I know she's okay. And you know what, Dawn? He answered me! Three times, in fact!"

"What do you mean, a sign? What kind of sign?" she wanted to know. Then Dave explained.

"Well, the first one came right after the accident. I was in our bed, and I was sleeping really soundly. All of a sudden I sat straight up. Then this force went through me, like a spirit. It was a good feeling, and somehow I just knew it was Kristin telling me she is okay. I felt really peaceful afterward," Dave told her.

"The next sign came a few days later. I was at one of my friend's house, and I was really restless. I just needed to go outside and take a walk. When I did, I looked up and noticed that the sky was full of different cloud formations. Suddenly, just as plain as day, this one cloud formed into a perfect teddy bear! You know how much Kristin loved teddy bears? I know it was God telling me that she is okay." Dawn hung on his every word with hope in her heart. Dave took a breath and continued.

"Then about a week later, I was watching 'our' show. You know, *Beverly Hills 90201*? It was one of the only shows that Kristin and I watched together. We loved it, and we never missed it. Anyway, it was Wednesday night and that show came on. It was the very last episode of the entire series. A wedding ceremony was taking place. It was really hard for me to watch. I just kept thinking she should be there with me. After the show was over, I went outside on the deck and looked up into the sky. There was a full moon and one small single cloud. All of a sudden that small cloud crossed in front of the moon, covering it completely. It was weird because the cloud was so small. Then the sky turned completely dark for a few seconds. The cloud then floated away, and the sky was bright again. I truly felt that God was telling me that my world was dark right now, but in time it would shine again. Three times He told me, Dawn. It's just us down here that are having a hard time without her because we miss her so much. But I know she's okay, and we'll see her again someday," he said confidently, hugging his sister–in–law tightly.

Dawn felt some relief after Dave's incredibly touching story. She didn't doubt for a minute that what he saw was real for him. But she desperately wanted to see some signs of her own. A few minutes later they both went to their rooms to get ready for the day's events.

For the next hour, Dave sat on his bed trying to compose yet another letter to his wife, one he could put inside the vault. He knew he wanted to write something, but the words just wouldn't come.

Suddenly, there was a knock on the door. It was the Project Manager from the accident, Steve Campbell. Over the past year, Steve had become a close family friend as well.

"I believe this belongs to you," he said, handing Dave some papers.

Dave recognized the bundle immediately. It was the letter to Kristin he had put inside the wine bottle the year before. For several seconds he was speechless.

"Where—how did you get this?" Dave finally asked.

"Some guy found the bottle laying on the beach

several miles from here. He apologized that he had to break it, but he didn't know how else to get inside. After he read the letter, he figured it had to do with the crash. It took him several months, but he was finally able to track me down through the airline," Steve explained.

"How long ago did he find it, do you know?"

"I believe he said he found it late last summer or early fall when he was jogging on the beach. He thought you might like to have it back."

Dave looked down at the letter again, but this time through very different eyes than when he first wrote it. What a difference a year makes, he thought to himself. Thank God for time.

"I didn't think I'd ever see this again. I guess I have my letter for the vault now. Let's go," he said, relieved that his problem had been solved.

Just after three o'clock in the afternoon, over 500 people gathered on the beach with their letters in hand, the sealed memories of days past written for their precious loved ones' eyes only. One by one they placed the letters into the large metal container. After the last one was inside, the vault was sealed and made ready for its journey out to sea.

The crowd then gathered into a circle. One person called out all eighty–eight names of the victims on board Flight 261. As each name was read, a bell was rung and a butterfly was set free. At 4:22 p.m., the exact time the plane went down, everyone in the circle held hands for a moment of silence. When the minute passed, the beautiful winged creatures fluttered about the shoreline before taking off to parts unknown as the wind carried them away.

The following day, the Coast Guard neared the sight of the accident, where their boat was greeted by over a half dozen gray whales. It was said that these whales migrated every year from Alaska to Puerto Vallarta, Mexico. Was it just coincidence that they were there? No one knows for sure. But it was, indeed, a perfect setting for the launching of the vault. The whales playfully jumped above the surface, while spurting water from their spouts. Shortly thereafter, the sealed vault was lowered into the 650–foot waters just off the coast of Anacapa Island, where Flight 261 had met its destiny. There the vault would remain forever.

Chapter Fifteen
SUMMARY

After weeks of searching the entire area, no survivors were found. The crash claimed the lives of all 88 people on board Flight 261. It took the authorities nearly a year to get all the rubble, personal items, and bits of airplane from the sea. The largest plane section recovered was less than ten feet across, because of the strong G-forces as the plane hit the water, going from hundreds of miles an hour to zero on impact!

The National Transportation Safety Board (NTSB) announced almost three years later that the cause of the crash was due to the lack of lubricant in the horizontal stabilizer. Because the pilots insisted on staying over the water, no other lives were lost except those on board. They fought to the very end, and they both died heroes.

All the passengers aboard were eventually recovered and identified, except for three: Anjesh (A.J.) Prasad from Seattle, Coriander Clemetson, and Kristin Mills. In fact, nothing of Kristin's was ever found—not a suitcase, nor a purse, nor cell phone—nothing to show that she had ever been on the plane. Dawn and her parents clung to a sense of hope for quite a while praying that maybe Kristin somehow missed the flight. But deep down they knew the truth. Kristin was never coming back.

This story of the "angel among us" is based on actual facts. There was no one left to tell what really happened on the plane that day. What is written here is only a theory taken from facts provided by family members and friends. But anyone who knew Kristin knows that she was not only working for Alaska Airlines that day, but also doing God's work bringing as many people to Him as possible in those last few moments before the jetliner disappeared from the sky.

God's presence was there that day, though no one knows for sure how many people actually took His hand in those last few seconds before the plane hit the water. No one, that is, except God Himself. But it is certain that 26–year–old

Kristin Rochelle Batdorf Mills was among those who did. For she truly believed that Jesus died for her sins and rose again. Jesus said, "I am the Resurrection and the Life. He who believes in Me will live, even though he dies; and whoever lives and believes in Me will never die. Do you believe this?" (John 11:25–26).

During those last few moments of her life, Kristin never once took her eyes off Jesus, just like Peter when he walked on water in Matthew 14:29. Peter was in the boat with other disciples when he saw Jesus walking on the water toward them. At first they were afraid, but then Peter saw that it was Jesus, and asked Him to command that he come and walk on the water with Him. And for as long as Peter kept his eyes on Jesus, he was not afraid. Like Peter, Kristin needed only to keep her eyes on Jesus.

For many confusing years, Kristin strayed out of bounds and away from God. But she always came back long enough to remember that He was the Way, the Truth, and the Life. Her trust and faith in His will for her was never a question of doubt. The promise of Proverbs 3:5–6—"Trust in the Lord with all your heart; do not depend on your own understanding. Seek His will in all you do, and He will direct your path"—was fulfilled in Kristin's life.

The family of Joe and Linda Knight knows that they were also among the people who willingly and openly went to the arms of the Lord. Because Joe and Linda were obedient to do His work on earth and believed in Jesus Christ, God was there for them when the time came for them to go home. Jesus tells us, "I am the Way and the Truth and the Life. No one comes to the Father except through Me" (John 14:6). The Knights believed in Jesus and God rewarded their faithfulness with eternal life in heaven. In 1 John 5:13, we are told, "These things I have written to you who believe in the name of the Son of God, that you may know that you have eternal life, and that you may continue to believe in the name of the Son of God."

The Bible is clear on what God expects from us. In Ephesians 2:10, Paul writes that "It is God Himself who has made us what we are and given us new lives from Christ Jesus; and long ages ago He planned that we should spend these lives helping others." We are all here for one reason: for His purpose, to bring Him the glory He so richly deserves. God "saved us and chose us for His holy work, not because we deserved it but because that was His plan" (2 Timothy 1:9).

Our sufferings and trials are meant to bring us closer to God, enabling us to know Him better and to seek His will. In the face of trials, rather than fall into despair, the Bible says we ought to "Consider it pure joy, my brothers, whenever you face trials of many kinds, because you know that the testing of faith develops perseverance" (James 1:2–3).

You can be sure that we will all have struggles, challenges, and even tragedy during our lifetime. And temptation is a certainty that is bound to make us stray. But if we keep our eyes fixed on Jesus and follow God's plan, we can and will get through it all. God never allows the tests we face to be greater than the grace He gives us to handle them, for as Paul writes in 1 Corinthians 10:13, "No temptation has overtaken you except such as is common to man; but God is faithful, who will not allow you to be tempted beyond what you are able, but with the temptation will also make the way of escape, that you may be able to bear it."

Chapter Sixteen
Kristin's Family Today

There isn't a day that goes by that Gene and Leslie Batdorf don't think about their daughter. It's still hard for them to believe that Kristin is never coming back. Though the pain has eased up somewhat, they are realistic enough to know that it may never truly be gone.

Since his daughter's accident, Gene refuses to get on an airplane. He drives or takes a train wherever he needs to go, no matter how far away it may be. Being on board any airplane would bring back too many unpleasant memories for him. He isn't ready to relive that kind of pain, and he is well aware that he may never be.

A few days after the accident, the family drove to Seattle to gather Kristin's personal things from her rented room. As soon as she opened the bedroom door, Leslie's eyes went directly to the Bible on the nightstand. She was taken aback, as it wasn't what she expected, not from Kristin anyway. When Leslie got closer she recognized it immediately. It was the same Bible Kristin had at the church camp when she was a little girl many years before. And it was still being used! A gentle smile caressed her lips.

As she turned the pages, looking for any sign of Kristin's existence within, Leslie came across a date and message just inside the cover. It was signed by Kristin herself. Relief flooded her heart, as tears of joy filled her eyes. "Thank you, Jesus!" she whispered. Written in pencil in the handwriting of a child were the day, date, and place that Kristin brought Jesus into her life. Her question was finally answered—Kristin had been ready to go!

The Batdorfs continue to find solace and comfort in knowing that Kristin is safe in Heaven with their Heavenly Father. It makes it easier to accept her absence. But they would still rather have had her here with them, at least for a little while longer.

Gene and Leslie trust God to provide them with the strength they need each day to get through their loss, as well as anything else this world might have for them. "I can do all things through Christ who strengthens me" (Philippians 4:13). This they know is true.

As for Dave Mills, his faith and trust in God prevailed. He left Las Vegas on April 27, 2001, and moved to Anchorage, Alaska. And just like God promised, the darkness around him lifted and his world turned bright again.

He and Aimee Harvey began a special friendship that lasted more than a year. It soon blossomed into love. They were married on November 10, 2001. Exactly one year and one day later their son, Hayden, was born.

Everyone heals in his or her own time, in his or her own way. Dawn Germain is no different. She struggles with her loss everyday, but it gets better with each sunrise. There is still a piece of her that is missing. It probably always will be. But she knows that her sister's laughter, love, and unforgettable smile are only a memory away. She only needs to close her eyes, and Kristin is there with her once again.

In the beginning, Dawn tried to blame God for Kristin's accident, though she never meant to. She was just so confused and so terribly hurt. She knows better than to ever think He would or could do that to anyone. He isn't that kind of a God. "He who does not love, does not know God; for God is love" (1 John 4:8). Because God is love, she knows He is a good God. She is certain that He was there for Kristin when she needed Him the most at that final moment when she took her last breath of life on earth.

Dawn is also certain that someday she and Kristin will be together again. In the meantime, she will move forward in her walk, making it stronger and more determined. Dawn knows God has a plan for her too. And she is willing and ready to do whatever it is. In His time, His will shall be done. She patiently awaits His call.

"For to me, to live is Christ and to die is gain. If I am to go on living in the body, this will mean fruitful labor for me. Yet what shall I choose? I do not know! I am torn between the two: I desire to depart and be with Christ, which is better by far" (Philippians 1: 21–23). Dawn knows that Kristin is in a much better place now. But she still has trouble convincing her heart. Time has been her best friend lately. As it slowly passes, so, too, does the pain.

God has graciously given to all of us so many wonderful things in this world. One of them is time. The passing of time helps us endure the tests we must face during our life here on earth. "For everything there is a season. A time for every purpose under heaven: A time to be born, and a time to die… A time to kill, and a time to heal… A time to weep, and a time to laugh… A time to mourn, and a time to dance" (Ecclesiastes 3:1–4).

Kristin knew it was her time to go. Thank God she was ready. He offered her His hand and she went willingly, joyfully and courageously. On her way she took some friends home with her. It was His plan.

With the sun on her face and the wind in her hair, Kristin Mills will forevermore be "blue side up," where she will dance in the clouds forever.

Lift up your eyes on high,

And see who has created these things,

Who brings out their host by number;

He calls them all by name,

By the greatness of His might

And the strength of His power;

Not one is missing.

(Isaiah 40:26)

Kristin's Photo Album

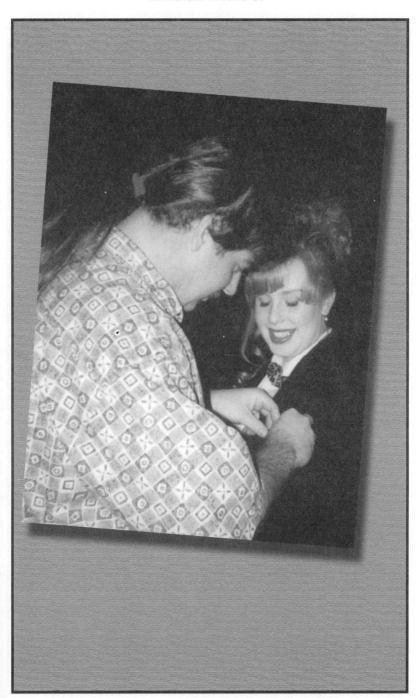

KRISTIN ROCHELLE BATDORF MILLS
1/11/1974 — 1/31/2000

OTHER BOOKS BY T.J. MARTINI

Wings of Pride:
The Story of Reno Air and Its People (2001)

Joe's Bible:
A Teen's Journey to Salvation (2003)

Standing on the Edge of Eternity (2005)

Destruction of Innocence:
A Mother's Guilt – A Daughter's Shame (Summer 2005)

To help you through your struggles or to learn more about Jesus Christ, visit our Web Site at www.justfaith.com. If you have any comments or stories you want to share you can contact TJ at *tjmartini@justfaith.com*